This Book Belongs To:

_____

The Rand McNally Book of
Favorite
Farm Animals

RAND McNALLY & COMPANY · Chicago

Established in 1856

CONTENTS

Farm Pets

Kitty, Kitty,
drinking milk,
Your fur is fine
and soft as silk.

My black hen
lays an egg each day
And cackles the news
as she walks away.

This woolly
little lamb
you see
Likes to run
and play with me.

"Hee-haw! Hee-haw!"
the donkey brays.
"My ears are long,"
is what he says.

Bossy eats grass
and swishes her tail
And gives us milk
in the shiny, big pail.

Billy Goat,
Billy Goat,
can't butt me
Because I stand
behind a tree.

Skippy drives the cows
and sheep
And over the fence
will lightly leap.

He wiggles his nose
and pretty pink ears—
I wonder what
my bunny hears.

Rex rides us
on his back at night
When work is done
and food's in sight.

Ducky, Ducky,
waddles by
And keeps her
pretty feathers dry.

Piggy, Piggy,
eats all day
And sleeps so much
he will not play.

But of all the pets,
the one I'd pick
Is the fuzzy little
yellow chick.

Chatterduck

Cats say MEE-OW—
Dogs say BOW-WOW—
Cows say MOO-OO—
And ducks say QUACK!

But little Chatterduck said
QUACK-QUACK-QUACK!
Chatterduck just loved
to hear himself talk.

He started to quack
when he woke up,
and he said
QUACK-QUACK-QUACK
all day long.

Chatterduck said
QUACK-QUACK-QUACK
while he ate.

He said QUACK-QUACK-QUACK while he swam.

He even said
QUACK-QUACK-QUACK
in his sleep, until—
The other ducks pushed him
right out of the duck house.

Poor Chatterduck
quacked himself
to sleep on a stump.

When he woke up
the next morning,
Chatterduck said
QUACK-QUACK-QUACK,
and he kept on
saying it all day.

The other ducks grew
very tired of hearing
Chatterduck say
QUACK-QUACK-QUACK,

The cat was tired of it—
The dog was tired of it—
And so were the cows
and all the other animals.

But Chatterduck
wasn't tired of it.
He loved to say
QUACK-QUACK-QUACK!

Then all the animals on
the farm got together.
The cow mooed—
The horses neighed—
The birds chirped—

The cat meowed–
The dog barked–
The ducks quacked–
The hens cackled–

The pigs squealed—
The turkey gobbled—
The frogs croaked—
The mice squeaked—
The bees buzzed—

The geese hissed—
And the farmer
and his wife
shouted BOO!

They made such
a tremendous noise
that everyone came running
from the village
to see what had happened.

But Chatterduck
didn't make a sound.
He just rushed to the woods
and hid his head in a hollow
log to get away from the noise.

After that day,
Chatterduck didn't like
noises much.
And he never, never said
QUACK-QUACK-QUACK again—

But when he had something
that was really worth
talking about—
He just said
QUACK.

This little white
Shetland, 'tis plain
to see,
Is just the right size
for Nancy Lee.

Star has a white mark
on her pretty
brown face,
She trots round
the track and goes
back to her place.

Sox has a brown coat,
but his feet
are snow-white,
I wonder if he
has to wash them
each night?

This little pony
likes to eat
An apple or carrot
because it's sweet.

Saddle and stirrups,
bridle and bit!
Duke is all ready.
Whose turn is it?

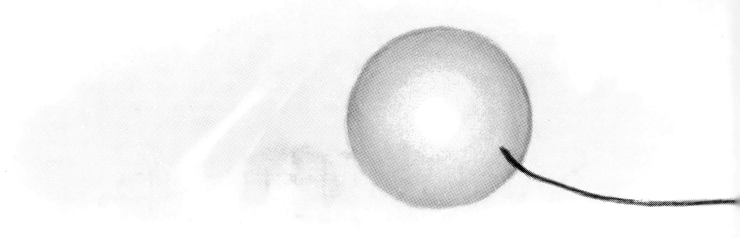

A Welsh pony is
so big and strong
He carries two boys
as he trots along.

Old Ben is fat
and dapple-gray,
He walks so slow
it takes him all day.

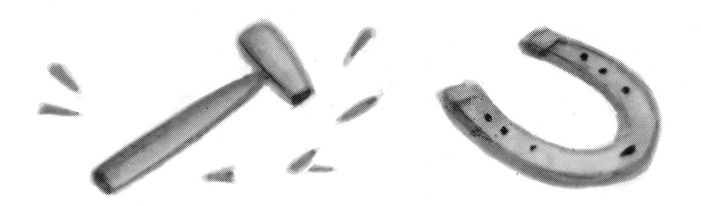

Big Ned's iron shoes
are strong and neat,
The blacksmith
nailed them
to his feet.

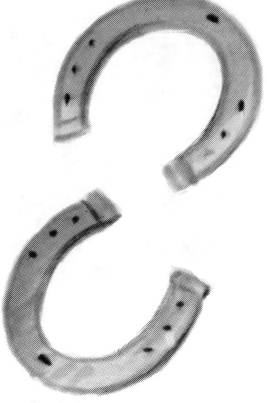

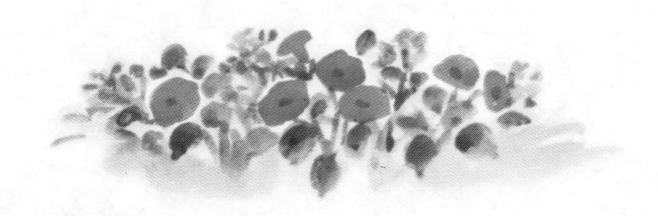

Belle is hitched
  to a little blue cart,
And as soon as
  you're seated,
  she's ready to start.

Crybaby Calf

Hiram the farmer was cheerful, even when a bee stung him.

Martha his wife was cheerful,
even when she slipped
and fell into the pond.

Jerry the horse was cheerful,
even when he caught his tail
in the door.

And the pigs were cheerful—
Except when dinner was late.

But the Crybaby Calf
was NEVER cheerful.
He cried almost all the time.

In the summer he cried
because it was hot—

And in the winter he cried
because it was cold.

One day he cried so much
that a pool of tears
formed all around him.

It was so cold
that the tears froze,
and the Crybaby Calf was
stuck fast to the ground!

Hiram the farmer tried to chop
him free with a hatchet.

Martha his wife tried
to melt him loose
with a kettle of warm water.

Jerry the horse
and Hiram the farmer
pulled at the calf
until they had to stop,
because it hurt—
And that made the calf cry
more than ever.

But when Hiram the farmer
and Martha his wife
got down on their knees—

And tried to melt the ice
by blowing on it,
they looked so funny—

That the Crybaby Calf
stopped crying
and laughed.
He laughed so hard
that he burst the ice
all around him
into little bits.
Then he jumped up on his feet
and pranced away.
And after that
the Crybaby Calf
was cheerful.

He didn't cry
when it was hot—
He didn't cry
when it was cold.

But for a long time afterward
he ALWAYS cried—
When he sat down.

Farm Animals

The silo's filled
   with stalks of corn,
The barn is stacked
   with hay.
The farmer's up at sunrise
To start the busy day.

But first to rise is rooster,
And *he* wakes all the rest,
Crowing at the crack
   of dawn,
He struts his puffed-out chest.

Mother Hen sits
on her eggs
And waits for them to hatch.
After baby chicks appear
They soon can peck and
scratch.

Fluffy puppies play and sleep,
And eat and sleep and play.
Barking back at screeching
 hawks,
They joyfully pass the day.

Mother Pig is counting out
The curly tails and "squeals."
Her piggies wallow
   in the mud—
They like the way it feels.

Ducks and geese
  like swimming,
They dive and splash around.
They smoothly glide
  through water—
But they *waddle* on the
  ground.

The little colt is gently
trained
By being quietly "told."
He's not allowed
    to give us rides
Until he's *two* years old.

The farmer keeps his rabbits
In a cozy, straw-filled hutch.
He feeds them hay and grain
  and greens,
And the salt they need
  so much.

The cows are in the pasture
"Mooing" deep and low.
It's time again for milking
Before the sun's last glow.

It's quiet on the farm
at night
When the busy day is done;
The crickets make the
only sounds
Till the rising of the sun.